Christmas in Florida

KAYLA LOWE

More of My Books

<u>Series</u>

<u>Christmas Blessings</u>

<u>Christmas Miracle for Two</u>
<u>A Christmas Promise of Love</u>
<u>A Christmas of Renewed Faith</u>

<u>Women of the Bible Fiction</u>

<u>Ruth</u>
<u>Esther</u>
<u>Rachel</u>
<u>Hannah</u>
<u>Deborah</u>

<u>Charms of the Chaste Court</u>

A Courtship in Covent Garden
Whispers in Westminster
Romance in Regent's Park
Serenade on Strand Street
Treasure in Tower Bridge

<u>Sweet Honey by the Sea</u>

<u>The Beekeeper's Secret (Book 1)</u>
<u>A Royal Honeycomb (Book 2)</u>
<u>Bees in Blossom (Book 3)</u>
<u>Honeyed Kisses (Book 4)</u>
<u>Blooming Forever (Book 5)</u>

<u>Strawberry Beach Series</u>

<u>Beachside Lessons (Book 1)</u>
<u>Beachside Lessons (Book 2)</u>
<u>Beachside Lessons (Book 3)</u>

Panama City Beach Series

Sun-Kissed Secrets (Book 1)
Sun-Kissed Secrets (Book 2)
Sun-Kissed Secrets (Book 3)

The Tainted Love Saga

Of Love and Deception (Book 1)
Of Love and Family (Book 2)
Of Love and Violence (Book 3)

Of Love and Abuse(Book 4)
Of Love and Crime (Book 5)
Of Love and Addiction (Book 6)
Of Love and Redemption (Book 7)

<u>Standalones</u>

Maiden's Blush

<u>Poetry</u>

Phantom Poetry
Lost and Found

Chapter One

Jenna gazed out the airplane window as the Florida coastline came into view, a patchwork of blue ocean and sandy shores. She let out a long sigh, feeling the weight of the past year in New York settle heavily on her shoulders.

As the plane touched down, Jenna gathered her carry-on bag and made her way through the bustling airport. The warm, humid air enveloped her as she stepped outside, a stark contrast to the crisp December chill she'd left behind in Manhattan.

Jenna walked to the rental car lot, her thoughts drifting to the life she'd built in the city—the long hours at the office, the high-pressure deals, the endless social engagements that left her feeling more disconnected than ever. When had she lost sight of what truly mattered?

The drive to her childhood home was a blur of familiar sights—the old movie theater where she'd had her first date, the park where she'd played countless games of tag, the church where she'd once found solace and purpose. As she turned onto her parents' street, a lump formed in her throat.

There it was, the old Livingston house, looking like something out of a Hallmark movie. Twinkling lights adorned the eaves, a wreath hung on the red front door, and the palm trees were all lit up with Christmas lights. Jenna parked the car and took a deep breath before grabbing her suitcase from the trunk.

As she approached the porch, the front door swung open, and there stood her mother, Marianne, a vision of warmth and love. "Jenna, sweetheart! Welcome home!" Marianne exclaimed, rushing forward to wrap her daughter in a tight embrace.

Jenna melted into her mother's arms, feeling the tension begin to ease from her body. "Hi, Mom," she murmured, breathing in the familiar scent of vanilla and cinnamon. "It's good to be back."

Marianne pulled back, her eyes shining with

happy tears. "Oh, just look at you! My beautiful girl, all grown up and taking on the world."

Jenna managed a small smile. "Not sure I'm doing such a great job of that lately," she admitted, her gaze dropping to the ground.

Marianne touched her daughter's cheek gently. "Everyone goes through tough times, honey. That's why faith and family are so important. They help guide us back to what really matters."

Jenna nodded, blinking back tears of her own. As she followed her mother inside, memories came flooding back—the sound of her father's laughter from the living room, the smell of freshly baked cookies, the warmth of the fireplace on a chilly evening.

Hey, believe it or not, Florida got chilly—even by the beach, so they had a small fireplace to knock the chill off.

The house was just as she remembered, every inch decorated for the holidays. The Christmas tree stood tall in the corner, not yet decorated though. That was a family tradition they all did together.

Garlands of coastal rope net draped across the mantel, and the nativity scene her grandmother had passed down took pride of place on the sideboard.

Jenna moved through the rooms as if in a dream, running her fingers along familiar surfaces, taking in the love and care her mother had poured into every detail. In that moment, surrounded by the trappings of her childhood, Jenna felt a flicker of something she'd thought long lost—a sense of belonging, of purpose, of faith.

Maybe, just maybe, coming home was exactly what she needed to find herself again.

The next morning, Jenna awoke to the aroma of freshly brewed coffee and sizzling bacon. She padded downstairs, still in her pajamas, to find her father at the stove, spatula in hand.

"There's my little girl," he said, his eyes crinkling as he smiled. "Just in time for breakfast."

Jenna hugged him tight, breathing in the familiar scent of his aftershave. "Thanks, Dad. It smells amazing."

As they ate, her parents chattered about the upcoming Christmas festivities—the town parade, the church nativity play, the annual cookie exchange. Jenna listened, a small smile playing on her lips, but her mind was miles away.

After breakfast, she pulled on a light hoodie and set out to explore the town square. The air slightly cool—not cold enough for a full coat but not warm enough for short sleeves either.

Main Street was a picture-perfect postcard of holiday cheer. Garlands of evergreen and twinkling lights adorned every storefront, and a giant Christmas tree stood in the center of the square, its branches heavy with ornaments.

Jenna paused before a window display of a toy train winding its way through a miniature village. She remembered standing in this very spot as a child, her nose pressed against the glass, dreaming of the day when she'd have a train set of her own.

A group of carolers stood on the corner, their voices rising in harmony as they sang "Silent Night." Jenna closed her eyes, letting the music wash over her. For a moment, she was transported back to her childhood, to the innocence and joy she'd once known.

As she wandered through the square, taking in the sights and sounds of the season, Jenna felt a pang of nostalgia so sharp it was almost painful. This was the life she'd left behind, the one she'd traded for the bright lights and big dreams of the city.

But standing there, surrounded by the warmth

and love of her hometown, Jenna couldn't help but wonder if she'd made the right choice. If, in chasing her ambitions, she'd lost something far more precious.

She shook her head, pushing the thought away. She had a life in New York, a career she'd worked hard for. She couldn't just walk away from that.

Jenna's reverie was broken by a familiar voice calling her name. She turned to see Alvin Bean, her high school sweetheart, striding towards her with a warm smile on his face.

"Jenna Livingston, as I live and breathe," he said, pulling her into a hug. "I heard you were back in town."

Jenna returned the embrace, surprised by the flood of emotions that washed over her at the sight of him. "Alvin, it's so good to see you."

He stepped back, holding her at arm's length. "Look at you, all fancy and citified. New York's been good to you."

Jenna laughed, tucking a stray lock of hair behind her ear. "It has its moments. But there's something to be said for the charm of a small town Christmas."

Alvin's eyes sparkled with mischief. "Careful, now. That sounds dangerously close to nostalgia."

"Maybe a little," Jenna admitted. "What about you? What have you been up to?"

"Oh, you know, the usual. Helping out at the church, volunteering with the community center." Alvin shrugged, his tone modest. "Just trying to make a difference where I can."

Jenna felt a pang of guilt. Here she was, chasing success in the big city, while Alvin was dedicating his life to serving others. "That's incredible, Alvin. I'm sure the community is lucky to have you."

He waved off the compliment. "It's nothing, really. Just doing what I can to spread a little light in the world."

As they talked, Jenna found herself drawn to the warmth and sincerity in Alvin's eyes. He had always been kind, but now there was a depth to him, a sense of purpose that she found both attractive and unsettling.

"Listen," Alvin said, his tone turning serious. "I know it's been a long time, but I was wondering if maybe you'd like to grab a coffee sometime? Catch up on old times?"

Jenna hesitated, torn between the pull of her past and the demands of her present. But looking into Alvin's hopeful face, she found herself nodding. "I'd like that."

Alvin's smile was like sunshine breaking through the clouds. "Great. I'll give you a call."

As he walked away, Jenna felt a flutter of excitement in her chest. Maybe coming home for Christmas wasn't such a bad idea after all.

Chapter Two

Jenna walked into the cozy church hall, the scent of pine and cinnamon filling the air. Her eyes scanned the room, heart skipping a beat when they landed on a familiar figure. Alvin looked up from the box of decorations he was sorting, a warm smile spreading across his face. "Jenna, I'm so glad you're here. We could really use an extra set of hands for the church's holiday outreach program this year. Would you be up for helping out while you're in town?"

Jenna hesitated, glancing down at her designer boots. Volunteering wasn't exactly on her agenda for this trip home. But as she met Alvin's hopeful gaze, old memories flooded back—late night talks about their dreams, laughter echoing in the church courtyard, the brush of his hand against hers. "I'd love to help," she found herself saying. "Just let me know what you need."

Alvin beamed. "That's the Jenna I remember—always ready to jump in and make a difference. I've missed that about you."

She ducked her head, feeling a blush creep into her cheeks. "Well, I've missed you too. It'll be nice to spend some time together again—I mean, you know, catching up and stuff."

"Definitely." His eyes twinkled with mischief. "Though I have to warn you, my gift wrapping skills haven't improved much since high school."

Jenna laughed, the awkwardness between them melting away. "I think I can handle that. We always did make a good team."

As they fell into easy conversation, sorting through decorations and reminiscing about Christmases past, Jenna felt a long-forgotten warmth blossoming in her chest.

Alvin handed Jenna a tangled string of lights, his fingers brushing against hers. A tingle ran up her arm at the contact. "Remember when we got stuck untangling these for hours back in high school?" he asked with a chuckle.

"How could I forget?" Jenna smiled, working at a

particularly stubborn knot. "We ended up covered in glitter and pine needles. My mom was finding tinsel in the couch cushions for weeks."

"But the church looked beautiful when we were done. Seeing everyone's faces light up at the Christmas Eve service made it all worth it." Alvin's eyes softened with the memory.

Jenna nodded, a wistful sigh escaping her lips. "Things seemed so much simpler then. I miss that feeling—of really being a part of something bigger than myself."

"You still can be, Jenna. That part of you, the part that cares deeply and wants to make a difference, it's still there." He placed a gentle hand on her shoulder. "Maybe this is a chance to reconnect with what really matters."

She met his gaze, seeing the sincerity and encouragement shining there. "Maybe you're right. I've been so focused on climbing the corporate ladder, I've lost sight of what truly fulfills me."

"Well, lucky for you, I happen to know a great place to start." Alvin grinned, gesturing around the church hall. "Plenty of opportunities to get involved and make a real impact right here."

Jenna laughed, shaking her head. "You always did have a way of putting things into perspective. Okay,

I'm in. Sign me up for whatever you need—gift wrapping, cookie baking, caroling, you name it."

"Careful, I might just take you up on that!" Alvin winked, warmth dancing in his eyes. "In all seriousness though, I'm really glad you're here, Jenna. It means a lot to me—to all of us."

As they continued working side by side, laughter and conversation flowing easily, Jenna felt a sense of peace and belonging settle over her. The twinkling lights cast a soft glow over the room, and the scent of pine and cinnamon wrapped around her like a comforting embrace.

For the first time in longer than she could remember, Jenna felt like she was exactly where she was meant to be. And as she stole glances at Alvin, admiring the way his strong hands carefully hung each ornament and the cute wrinkle of concentration on his brow, she couldn't help but wonder if maybe, just maybe, her heart was finally leading her home too.

Jenna sat on the edge of her childhood bed, staring at the faded posters on the wall. She couldn't shake the unsettled feeling that had been growing since she arrived home. The reunion with Alvin had stirred up more than just old memories—it had awakened a longing she thought she'd left behind years ago.

With a sigh, she reached for her Bible on the nightstand, running her fingers over the worn leather cover. When was the last time she'd opened it? In the constant hustle of her New York life, her faith had been pushed to the margins, relegated to a dusty corner of her heart.

"God, are you still there?" she whispered, her voice barely audible in the quiet room. "I feel so far away from you, from everything I used to believe in. What happened to me?"

The silence seemed to stretch on forever, broken only by the soft ticking of the clock on the wall. Jenna's thoughts drifted to her family, to the values they'd instilled in her since childhood. Kindness, compassion, putting others before herself—somehow, those things had gotten lost in her relentless pursuit of success.

A knock on the door startled her from her reverie. "Jenna, honey?" her mother called. "We're about to start decorating the tree. Come join us!"

Jenna took a deep breath, tucking her Bible under her arm as she stood. "Coming, Mom!"

Downstairs, the living room was a flurry of activity. Her father wrestled with a tangled string of lights, while her younger sister sorted through boxes of ornaments. The scent of pine and cinnamon filled the air, mingling with the soft strains of Christmas carols on the radio.

"There you are!" her mother exclaimed, handing her a shimmering glass bauble shaped like a seahorse. "I was just telling your sister about the year you insisted on putting all the ornaments on the bottom half of the tree because you couldn't reach any higher."

Jenna laughed, the memory warming her from the inside out. "I was what, five years old? I thought it looked perfect."

As she hung the ornament on a branch, she felt a sense of belonging wash over her. This was what she'd been missing—the simple joys of family, the comfort of traditions that connected her to something bigger than herself.

Her father draped an arm around her shoulders, pulling her close. "It's good to have you home, sweetheart. Christmas just isn't the same without you."

Jenna leaned into his embrace, blinking back sudden tears. "I've missed this," she admitted. "I've missed all of you."

As they continued to decorate the tree, laughter

and stories flowing easily, Jenna felt a flicker of hope reignite in her heart. Maybe it wasn't too late to find her way back—back to her faith, back to the person she used to be.

And maybe with God's love guiding her, she could finally discover where she truly belonged.

Chapter Three

J enna stepped into the church hall, a box of decorations balanced precariously in her arms. The scent of pine and cinnamon filled the air, mingling with the soft strains of Christmas carols playing in the background.

"Need a hand with that?" Alvin's deep voice startled her, and she nearly dropped the box.

"Alvin! I didn't see you there." Jenna smiled, grateful as he took the heavy box from her. "Thanks. I thought I could manage on my own, but I guess I overestimated my strength."

Alvin chuckled, setting the box down on a nearby table. "No worries. That's what I'm here for." His blue eyes sparkled with warmth as he surveyed the hall. "Looks like we've got our work cut out for us, huh?"

Jenna nodded, taking in the bare walls and undecorated tables. "I can't believe how much there is to do. Where do we even start?"

"How about with the tree?" Alvin suggested, gesturing to a towering evergreen in the corner. "It's the centerpiece of the whole thing. Once we get that done, the rest will fall into place."

As they began to string lights and hang ornaments, Jenna found herself relaxing in Alvin's presence. There was something about him that put her at ease, his calm demeanor and gentle humor a balm to her frayed nerves.

"So, tell me about your life in the city," Alvin prompted, carefully placing a shimmering star on a branch. "What's it like being a hotshot executive?"

Jenna laughed, shaking her head. "It's not nearly as glamorous as it sounds. Mostly, it's just a lot of long hours and high-pressure meetings." She paused, considering. "But I love the challenge of it, you know? The feeling of accomplishment when you close a big deal or land a new client."

Alvin nodded, his expression thoughtful. "I can understand that. But don't you ever miss the slower pace of life? The chance to just breathe and enjoy the moment?"

Jenna sighed, her fingers brushing against a delicate glass ornament. "Sometimes, I do. Especially when I come back home and see how different everything is here. It's like stepping into another world."

"But that's the beauty of it, isn't it?" Alvin's voice was soft, his gaze distant. "Having a place to come back to, a place that grounds you and reminds you of what really matters."

Jenna studied him, struck by the depth of his words. "You make it sound so simple."

Alvin smiled, meeting her eyes. "Maybe it is. Maybe we just have a way of complicating things that don't need to be complicated."

As they continued to work, their conversation flowed easily, moving from childhood memories to hopes for the future. Jenna found herself opening up in a way she hadn't in years, sharing her doubts and fears, her dreams and aspirations.

And as the hours passed and the church hall transformed into a winter wonderland, Jenna realized that something else was transforming, too. The connection between her and Alvin, once a fragile spark, was growing stronger with every shared laugh, every heartfelt confession.

As the last ornament was hung and the final strand of tinsel draped, Jenna stepped back to admire their handiwork. The church hall had been transformed into a glittering wonderland, the twinkling lights and shimmering decorations a testament to the magic of the season.

"We make a pretty good team, don't we?" Alvin grinned, draping an arm around her shoulders.

Jenna leaned into his touch, a contented sigh escaping her lips. "We always did. Some things never change, I guess."

Alvin's eyes softened, his gaze lingering on her face. "And some things do."

A comfortable silence settled between them, the air thick with unspoken emotions. Jenna's heart raced, her skin tingling where Alvin's arm rested.

"Hey, what do you say we take a break?" Alvin suggested, his voice breaking the spell. "We've been cooped up in here for hours. A little fresh air might do us good."

Jenna nodded, grateful for the chance to clear her head. "Lead the way."

They stepped outside, the crisp December air a welcome respite from the warmth of the church. The sun had begun to set, painting the sky in hues of lavender and gold.

"I've always loved this time of day," Alvin mused. "It's like the world is holding its breath, waiting for something magical to happen."

Jenna smiled, tucking her hands into her coat pockets. "You always did have a way with words. I remember you used to write the most beautiful poems back in high school."

Alvin ducked his head, a bashful grin tugging at his lips. "I can't believe you remember that. I was so nervous to show them to anyone, but you always encouraged me."

"Because I could see how talented you were, even then." Jenna bumped her shoulder against his. "You have a gift, Alvin. A way of seeing the world that most people miss."

They walked in comfortable silence for a moment, the only sound the crunch of snow beneath their feet. The houses lining the street were decked out in twinkling lights and garlands, each one a small beacon of holiday cheer.

"Can I ask you something?" Alvin's voice was hesitant, his gaze fixed on the ground.

Jenna's heart skipped a beat. "Of course. Anything."

"Do you ever wonder what might have happened

if we'd stayed in touch after high school? If we hadn't let life pull us in different directions?"

The question hung in the air between them, heavy with the weight of missed opportunities and unspoken regrets. Jenna swallowed hard, her throat suddenly tight. The question hung in the air between them, heavy with the weight of missed opportunities and unspoken regrets. She took a deep breath, gathering her courage. "I'd be lying if I said I hadn't thought about it. About us, and what might have been."

Alvin turned to face her, his blue eyes searching hers. "Jenna, I..."

But before he could continue, the shrill ring of Jenna's phone shattered the moment. She fumbled in her pocket, a flush rising to her cheeks. "I'm sorry, I have to take this. It's work."

Alvin nodded, understanding etched in his features. "Of course. I'll give you some privacy."

As he walked a few paces away, Jenna pressed the phone to her ear, her heart still racing. "Jenna Livingston speaking."

The voice on the other end launched into a barrage of questions and demands, pulling Jenna back into the high-pressure world she'd left behind in New York. She listened intently, her brow furrowed in concentration.

Several minutes later, she ended the call with a heavy sigh. Alvin approached, concern in his eyes. "Everything okay?"

Jenna forced a smile. "Just a minor crisis at the office. Nothing I can't handle." She tucked her phone away, trying to recapture the magic of the moment. "Where were we?"

But the spell had been broken, the intimacy of their conversation lost to the intrusion of the outside world. They walked back to the church in silence, each lost in their own thoughts.

As they said their goodbyes, Alvin's hand lingered on Jenna's arm. "Have a great evening, Jenna."

She smiled at him. "You too, Alvin."

With a final squeeze of her hand, he turned and walked away, leaving Jenna alone with her thoughts. She watched him go, a sense of longing and uncertainty swirling within her.

Chapter Four

Sunlight streamed through the stained-glass windows of the small church, casting a kaleidoscope of colors across the wooden pews. Alvin stood at the pulpit, his blue eyes shining with conviction as he addressed the congregation. "This holiday season, let us remember the true meaning of Christmas—to love and serve one another, just as Christ loved and served us."

Jenna sat in the back row, her hazel eyes fixed on Alvin. She couldn't help but admire his dedication to his faith and his community. After the service ended, Jenna approached him with a warm smile. "That was a beautiful message, Alvin. You really have a gift for inspiring people."

Alvin ducked his head humbly. "Thank you,

Jenna. But it's not about me—it's about letting God's love shine through each of us to make a difference." He gestured around the church. "This place, these people, serving the Lord—it's my calling. There's nothing else I'd rather devote my life to."

Jenna nodded, a wistful expression crossing her face as she glanced at the cheerful poinsettias lining the altar and the twinkling lights on the Christmas tree. Spending time back in her quaint Florida hometown had stirred up old dreams and desires she thought she had left behind. Visions flashed through her mind of a simpler life, filled with faith, family, and...

She shook her head. No, she had worked too hard to build her career in New York to walk away from it all now. The city was where she belonged, chasing her ambitions.

Wasn't it?

"You okay, Jenna?" Alvin asked gently, placing a comforting hand on her shoulder. His touch sent a tingle down her spine.

"Y-yes, I'm fine," she stammered, stepping back and smoothing her skirt. "I was just thinking about how different my life in the city is from all this." She waved her hand to indicate the church. "Sometimes I wonder..."

Alvin waited patiently, but Jenna struggled to find the right words. How could she tell him that part of her longed for the life she might have had if she had stayed, with him by her side? A life centered on faith, love, and serving others?

She forced a bright smile. "Never mind. I'm so impressed by your commitment to your church and community, Alvin. You're making such a positive impact here."

"Well, I couldn't do it without all the amazing volunteers," Alvin demurred. "Actually, I wanted to ask if you might be interested in helping with our outreach program while you're in town? We could really use an extra set of hands to prepare care packages and meals for families in need this Christmas."

Jenna hesitated, old insecurities and excuses bubbling up. She opened her mouth, intending to politely decline. But something in Alvin's hopeful expression stopped her. Maybe it was time she stepped out of her comfort zone and explored a different path—even if only for a little while.

"You know what? I'd love to help," she found herself saying. The words felt right as soon as she spoke them.

Alvin's face lit up, making Jenna's heart flutter.

"Wonderful! I just know you'll be a blessing to so many." He squeezed her hand.

As Jenna followed him to the church kitchen, she couldn't quiet the small voice inside whispering that maybe, just maybe, this was exactly where she was meant to be...

The church kitchen buzzed with activity as volunteers packed boxes and prepared hot meals. The savory aroma of turkey and stuffing mingled with the sweet scent of pumpkin pie, enveloping Jenna in a warm embrace. She tied an apron around her waist and joined Alvin at a table, assembling care packages filled with toiletries, warm socks, and heartfelt notes of encouragement.

As they worked side by side, Alvin shared stories of the families they were helping—single mothers struggling to make ends meet, elderly couples facing loneliness, and children who might not otherwise receive gifts this Christmas. Jenna felt a lump form in her throat, moved by the raw vulnerability in Alvin's voice.

"I can't imagine how difficult it must be," she

murmured, tucking a soft teddy bear into a box. "Facing the holidays with so little..."

Alvin nodded, his blue eyes glistening with empathy. "It's heartbreaking at times. But that's why faith is so important—it gives us hope and strength to keep going, even in the darkest moments."

Jenna paused, considering his words. "I admire your faith, Alvin. Truly. But sometimes I wonder...how do you keep believing when life is so hard?"

He smiled gently, reaching for her hand. "It's not always easy," he admitted. "I've had my own struggles and doubts. But in those moments, I cling to the truth that God's love never fails. He's with us in the valleys and on the mountaintops."

Jenna swallowed hard, something stirring deep within her soul. A longing for the peace and purpose Alvin seemed to possess. "I want that," she whispered. "To feel that sense of belonging and direction."

"It's never too late," Alvin assured her, his thumb brushing her knuckles. "Take one step at a time. Explore your faith. Surround yourself with people who lift you up. And know that I'm here for you, always."

Tears blurred Jenna's vision as she leaned into his comforting touch.

Alvin had always been so sure of himself—even as a gangly high school boy, but seeing him now, as a man with such conviction...

Jenna's heart skipped a beat.

As the day wore on, Jenna and Alvin loaded the care packages into cars and delivered them throughout the community. At each stop, Jenna witnessed the profound impact of their efforts. Grateful smiles, tearful hugs, and heartfelt prayers of thanks filled her with a joy she'd never experienced in the boardroom.

One particular encounter left an indelible mark on her heart. They visited a young family living in a cramped apartment, the parents weary but determined. As Jenna handed out stuffed animals to the wide-eyed children, the mother embraced her tightly.

"Thank you," she whispered fiercely. "You have no idea how much this means to us."

Jenna blinked back tears, her heart full to bursting. "It's my pleasure," she managed. "Truly."

On the drive back to the church, Alvin reached

over and squeezed Jenna's hand. "You were amazing today," he said softly.

She met his gaze, her eyes shining with newfound purpose. "I feel like I finally understand what I've been missing all these years. This sense of connection and meaning."

Alvin smiled, his expression tender. "Welcome home, Jenna."

As they pulled back into the parking lot and the volunteer day drew to a close, Jenna found herself lingering in the church hall, helping to tidy up the remnants of the day's activities. The laughter of children and the grateful smiles of parents played in her mind like a heartwarming melody, filling her with a sense of contentment she had never known before.

Alvin approached her, his eyes soft and understanding. "You're a natural at this, you know," he said, gesturing to the organized stacks of supplies. "The way you connected with those families today...it was truly something special."

Jenna ducked her head, a slight blush coloring her cheeks. "I didn't do anything extraordinary," she demurred. "I just listened and tried to show them that someone cares."

"And that, Jenna, is exactly what makes it extraordinary," Alvin replied, his voice warm with admiration. "In a world that often feels cold and indifferent, your kindness shines like a beacon of hope."

As they worked side by side, their hands brushed occasionally, sending little sparks of electricity through Jenna's veins. She found herself stealing glances at Alvin, marveling at the strength and gentleness that seemed to radiate from his very being.

Lost in thought, Jenna didn't notice the stack of boxes teetering precariously until it was too late. With a surprised yelp, she reached out to steady them, but Alvin was quicker. His strong arms encircled her, pulling her close as the boxes tumbled harmlessly to the floor.

For a moment, time seemed to stand still. Jenna's heart raced as she looked up into Alvin's eyes, their faces mere inches apart. In that instant, she saw a flicker of something deep and profound—a connection that went beyond mere friendship or shared faith.

Alvin cleared his throat, reluctantly releasing her from his embrace. "Careful there," he whispered, his usually confident demeanor giving way to a boyish shyness.

As they finished their tasks, stealing glances and

sharing shy smiles, Jenna felt a warmth blossoming in her chest.

Chapter Five

The warm glow of the stained glass windows cast a kaleidoscope of colors across the wooden pews as Jenna stepped into the church, the familiar scent of incense and polished oak enveloping her like a comforting embrace. She smiled softly, memories of Christmases past flooding her mind as she made her way down the aisle.

"Jenna, there you are!" Pastor Greer called out, waving her over to the front of the church where a small group had gathered. "We were just discussing the music for the Christmas Eve service."

Jenna joined the circle, nodding in greeting to the others. "I'd be happy to help out with the music, Pastor. What did you have in mind?"

"Well, we were thinking of incorporating some traditional carols, but also adding a few contemporary songs to appeal to the younger crowd. What do you think?" Pastor Greer looked at Jenna expectantly.

Jenna considered for a moment, her eyes drifting to the large wooden cross at the front of the church. "I think that's a great idea. We could even have a solo or duet performance to add a special touch."

"Excellent suggestion! Would you be willing to sing a solo, Jenna? Your voice has always been so beautiful," Mrs. Greer, the church organist, chimed in.

A blush crept up Jenna's cheeks as she smiled shyly. "I'd be honored. There's actually a song that's been on my heart lately...it reminds me of my childhood Christmases here."

Pastor Greer placed a gentle hand on her shoulder. "That sounds perfect, Jenna. Why don't you give us a little preview?"

Jenna took a deep breath and closed her eyes, the familiar melody flowing from her lips as she began to sing. The words spoke of hope, faith, and the joy of coming home for the holidays. As she sang, memories of decorating the Christmas tree with her family, baking cookies with her grandmother, and attending candlelight services flooded her mind.

The song ended and Jenna opened her eyes, blinking back the tears that had formed. The small group applauded, their faces filled with warmth and appreciation.

"That was beautiful, Jenna," Pastor Greer said softly. "I can tell that song holds a special place in your heart."

Jenna nodded, a sense of peace and belonging settling over her. Her eyes met Alvin's, and something in his gaze made her blush.

The way he was looking at her...

As the group continued to discuss the music selections, Jenna felt a renewed sense of connection to her faith and her roots. She knew that no matter where life took her, this little church would always be a place of nostalgia, healing, and coming home.

Mrs. Greer placed a stack of sheet music on the podium and invited everyone to grab a copy.

Alvin's fingers brushed against Jenna's as they reached for the sheet music simultaneously. A spark of electricity seemed to pass between them, and their eyes met, holding each other's gaze for a moment too long. The air grew thick with unspoken feelings, and Jenna felt her heart begin to race.

"I..." Alvin began, his voice barely above a whisper. "Jenna, I've been wanting to tell you..."

The sound of the church door swinging open broke the spell, and they jumped apart as if burned.

As they continued to practice, Jenna found it hard to concentrate, her mind constantly drifting to Alvin. What would have happened if they hadn't been interrupted? What was he going to say?

Were these feelings real, or just a result of the nostalgia and emotions stirred up by the music?

Later that evening, Jenna sat at the dinner table with her parents, pushing her food around her plate. Her mother's voice cut through her thoughts. "Jenna, your father and I have been talking. We're concerned about your future."

"What do you mean?" Jenna asked, setting down her fork.

Her father leaned forward, his brow furrowed. "We know you left behind a promising career in New York to come back here. But what about your long-term plans? Are you really going to be happy living so far away from home forever?"

Jenna sighed, the weight of their expectations

heavy on her shoulders. "I'm still figuring things out, Dad."

"We just want what's best for you, sweetheart," her mother said gently. "Don't forget about what's important."

Jenna's mother reached across the table, placing her hand over Jenna's. "You know, dear, we couldn't help but notice how you and Alvin were looking at each other during the rehearsal today." Her eyes sparkled with a knowing glint.

Heat rushed to Jenna's cheeks, and she ducked her head, suddenly finding her plate of mashed potatoes and gravy intensely interesting. "Mom, it's not like that. We're just friends."

Her father chuckled, leaning back in his chair. "Friends, huh? I seem to remember a time when you two were inseparable. Always running off together, sharing secrets and dreams."

"That was a long time ago, Dad," Jenna mumbled, pushing a piece of roast beef around her plate with her fork. "Things change."

"But some things never do," her mother said softly, a wistful smile on her face. "The way Alvin looks at you...it's the same way he did when you were teenagers. Like you're the only girl in the world."

Jenna's heart skipped a beat at her mother's

words, but she quickly pushed the feeling aside. "We're just working together on the Christmas Eve service, that's all. There's nothing more to it."

Her father exchanged a knowing glance with her mother, a mischievous twinkle in his eye. "If you say so, sweetheart. But don't be surprised if you find yourself under the mistletoe with a certain someone at the church Christmas party."

"Dad!" Jenna exclaimed, her face now a bright shade of crimson. She dropped her fork with a clatter, the sound echoing in the suddenly too-quiet dining room.

Her mother laughed, a light, tinkling sound that reminded Jenna of wind chimes in a gentle breeze. "Oh, leave the poor girl alone, John. Can't you see you're embarrassing her?"

Jenna pushed back her chair, the wooden legs scraping against the hardwood floor. "I think I'm going to head up to my room for a bit."

As she made her way up the creaky stairs, her parents' good-natured laughter followed her, mingling with the soft strains of Christmas carols drifting from the living room radio. Jenna closed the door to her childhood bedroom behind her, leaning against it with a heavy sigh.

Her gaze drifted to the window, where the twinkling lights of the neighbor's Christmas display cast a soft, multicolored glow across the sandy lawn. She watched the lights dance and flicker, her mind wandering to Alvin and the moment they had shared during the rehearsal.

Jenna knelt on the worn carpet of her childhood bedroom, her hands clasped tightly in front of her. The soft glow of the bedside lamp cast a warm light over her face as she closed her eyes and took a deep, steadying breath.

"Lord," she whispered, her voice trembling slightly, "I come to you seeking guidance and clarity. My heart is so confused right now."

She paused, gathering her thoughts as she listened to the gentle patter of rain against the window. "I thought I had it all figured out—my career, my life in New York. But being back here, surrounded by the love and warmth of this community...it's made me question everything."

Jenna's mind drifted to Alvin, and a small smile tugged at the corners of her mouth. "And then there's Alvin. When I'm with him, I feel something I've never felt before. It's like my soul is at peace, and everything just feels...right."

She sighed, her brow furrowing as she continued, "But is this really what you have planned for me,

God? Am I meant to leave behind everything I've worked for and start a new life here? Please, give me a sign. Show me the path you want me to take."

As Jenna sat in silent prayer, a sense of calm washed over her. The doubts and fears that had been swirling in her mind began to dissipate, replaced by a newfound sense of purpose and clarity.

Chapter Six

Jenna's heels clicked rapidly on the hardwood floor as she paced back and forth in the church community room, her brow furrowed. The usually comforting Christmas decorations seemed to mock her now. Alvin stood a few feet away, his hands clasped tightly.

"I can't believe you didn't tell me about this sooner," Jenna said, trying to keep her voice steady. "We're supposed to be partners on the Christmas charity drive. I thought we had an agreement."

Alvin sighed heavily. "I'm sorry, Jenna. I wasn't trying to keep anything from you. Things just got so busy with the toy drive that it slipped my mind to mention the change in plans. I should have communicated better."

Jenna stopped pacing and crossed her arms. "Well, now the budget is a mess and we'll have to scramble to make it work. If you had just talked to me first..." She shook her head. Jenna hated this kind of stress. It reminded her of what she dealt with in the city. She wasn't upset by the turn in plans more so than being blindsided by it all. "It's embarrassing when I'm insisting to the local nursery that we paid for fifty poinsiettas when we didn't. Do you know how incompetent that makes me look?"

"You're right," Alvin said quietly. "I made a mistake. Let me see what I can do to fix it." He reached out a tentative hand, but Jenna stepped back.

"I think...I just need some space right now," she said, her voice cracking slightly. "I'll figure out the budget on my own."

Alvin's shoulders slumped as Jenna brushed past him and out the door into the chilly evening air. Doubts swirled in her mind as she walked quickly to her car, blinking back tears.

Was she overreacting? No, Alvin should have included her in this decision. They were supposed to be a team. He's the one who'd asked for her help with all this.

Still, a twinge of regret gnawed at her for being so harsh with him.

Jenna got into her car and gripped the steering wheel tightly. The sting of the misunderstanding mingled with a deep sense of loneliness that the festive decorations along Beach Street did little to assuage.

As much as she loved her family, being back in her hometown made her question all the choices that led her to trade a white picket fence for a corner office in Manhattan. The trappings of success felt hollow in moments like these.

Jenna drove aimlessly, muscle memory taking her along back roads until she found herself at her favorite beach spot. She parked and got out, pulling her jacket tighter as she walked to the shore's edge.

Memories of summer barbecues and winter picnics in this very spot flashed through her mind—a lifetime of love and laughter with family, friends, and faith at the center of it all.

When had she let those priorities fall by the wayside?

She closed her eyes and listened to the tide crashing on the shoreline. Jenna no longer felt like a confident businesswoman, but a lost little girl very far from home. She closed her eyes and whispered a broken prayer. "God, I don't know if I'm on the right path anymore. Please guide me back to what really matters."

Only the sounds of the waves and a distant seagull answered in the growing darkness. Jenna shivered, the chill from the beach wind cutting through her.

No epiphanies came, only a bone-deep weariness and sense that she had strayed far from the person she wanted to be.

With a sigh, Jenna turned back to her car. Tonight there would be no easy answers, only fitful sleep and the ache of isolation, even in this town full of old friends and loving family. She could only hope that the light of a new day would illuminate the road ahead. Until then, she would have to rely on fragile faith to sustain her through the shadows of self-doubt.

Chapter Seven

When Jenna opened the door of her parents' home, her mom and dad were sitting on the couch together watching a movie. Jenna's mother looked up, her face etched with concern when she took in her daughter. "Jenna, honey, what's wrong?"

Her mother could always tell when something was wrong. Just one look at her face...

Jenna rushed into her mother's open arms, the warmth of the embrace a balm to her battered spirit. Tears she'd been holding back all night broke free as she sobbed against her mom's shoulder. "Everything's just such a mess. I don't know what to do anymore."

Her dad's strong hand rubbed soothing circles

on her back. "Whatever it is, Jenna-bug, you know we're here for you. Why don't we sit down and talk it through?"

Sandwiched between her parents, Jenna let them guide her onto the cozy familiarity of their living room couch. She sank onto the plush sofa, drawing the quilt her grandmother had made tightly around her shoulders. Mom pressed a steaming mug of hot cocoa into her hands before settling beside her.

"Now, tell us what's troubling you, sweetheart," Mom prompted gently.

The story poured out of Jenna in fits and starts —the misunderstanding with Alvin, her growing doubts about her career path, the gnawing sense that she'd lost sight of what truly mattered. "I just feel so lost," she admitted, staring into the swirling depths of her tea. "Like I don't know who I am anymore. I don't know if God even hears me anymore."

Her father leaned forward, weathered hands clasped between his knees. "Jenna, do you remember what Pastor Greer always says? 'We're never lost when we walk with the Lord.' You may have strayed a bit from the path, but God is always there to guide you back."

Mom nodded, her eyes shimmering with empathy and wisdom. "Your dad's right, honey. I know it feels overwhelming right now, but you're not alone. You have your faith, and you have us. We'll support you, no matter what."

Jenna managed a wobbly smile, her heart lightening a fraction. "I don't know what I'd do without you both."

"Well, lucky for you, you'll never have to find out," Dad declared, his mustache twitching with a grin. "Now, what do you say we break out the board games like old times? I'll even let you be the racecar in Monopoly."

A surprised laugh bubbled up in Jenna's throat, the first genuine one in days. "You're on, old man. Prepare to eat my dust."

As her parents bustled about setting up the game, their good-natured bickering washing over her, Jenna breathed a little easier. The path ahead might be uncertain, but at least she knew she wouldn't have to walk it alone.

Later that night, Jenna found herself on the back porch swing with her mother, a worn quilt shared across their laps. Moonlight painted the garden in soothing silver as crickets sang their nightly serenade.

"Mom?" Jenna's voice was hushed in the intimate darkness. "How did you know Daddy was the one? That you were following God's plan for your life?"

Her mother was quiet for a moment, her profile limned in lunar glow as she gathered her thoughts. "It wasn't a single moment of clarity, more like...a thousand little ones. When I was with your father, I felt a deep sense of peace. Like my soul was at home."

Jenna nodded slowly, chewing on her bottom lip. "But what if I never feel that? What if I'm too focused on worldly success to recognize it?"

Mom's hand found hers beneath the quilt, her fingers rough with years of love and labor. "Oh, honey. We all get distracted by the world sometimes. The key is to keep turning back to God. He'll never steer you wrong."

"I want to trust in that, I do. It's just hard when everything feels so uncertain."

"Faith isn't about having all the answers. It's about believing in the One who does." Mom's smile was gentle in the moonlight. "When I was your age, I had so many doubts and questions. But I kept praying, kept seeking God's guidance. And you know what? He led me to your father, to the life we built together. It wasn't always easy, but it was always worth it."

Jenna rested her head on her mother's shoulder, breathing in the comforting scent of lavender and home. "I want a love like that. One that weathers the storms and grows stronger."

"You'll find it, sweetheart. Just keep your heart open and your eyes fixed on the Lord. He has a beautiful plan for you, even if you can't see it yet."

There in the stillness of the night, enfolded in her mother's love and the whisper of divine promise, Jenna felt the first stirrings of hope. Perhaps the misunderstandings and missteps were all part of a greater tapestry—one she couldn't yet glimpse in full, but could trust was being woven with care by a Master's hand.

With a sigh of contentment, Jenna snuggled closer to her mom, letting the creaking lullaby of the porch swing soothe her troubled heart. Tomorrow would bring its own challenges, its own opportunities for growth and grace. But for now, she was exactly where she needed to be. Held fast by the unshakable pillars of faith and family, ready to face whatever lay ahead.

Chapter Eight

Jenna's fingers hovered over her phone, Alvin's number glowing on the screen. She took a deep breath, the crisp morning air filling her lungs with a renewed sense of purpose. The gentle rustling of the oak trees seemed to whisper encouragement, their leaves dancing in the golden sunlight that filtered through her bedroom window.

"Here goes nothing," she murmured, pressing the call button. Her heart raced as the phone rang once, twice. On the third ring, Alvin's warm voice filled her ear.

"Jenna! What a pleasant surprise." His tone held a mixture of genuine delight and a hint of uncertainty.

"Alvin, hi. I hope I'm not catching you at a bad

time." Jenna twirled a lock of hair around her finger, a nervous habit she thought she'd outgrown.

"Not at all. I always have time for you." The sincerity in his words made her feel even guiltier for snapping at him the other day.

"I was hoping we could meet up and talk. About..." She paused, gathering her courage before she finished with, "everything."

There was a brief silence on the other end, and Jenna could almost picture Alvin's thoughtful expression. "I'd like that, Jenna. How about we meet at the park by the old willow tree? Say, in an hour?"

"Perfect. I'll see you there." Jenna ended the call, a flicker of hope igniting in her chest.

An hour later, Jenna found herself beneath the sprawling branches of the willow tree, its cascading leaves creating a serene, almost magical atmosphere. She spotted Alvin approaching, his stride confident yet relaxed.

"Hey there, stranger," he greeted her with a lopsided grin that made her heart skip a beat.

"Hey yourself." Jenna returned the smile, feeling the tension between them start to dissipate. "Thanks for meeting me."

"Of course. I've been wanting to talk to you too."

Alvin's blue eyes met hers, filled with a mixture of warmth and apprehension.

They settled on the grass, the soft rustling of leaves providing a soothing backdrop. Jenna took a deep breath, ready to pour her heart out and mend the rift between them.

"Alvin, I'm sorry I snapped at you the other day," she said, her voice wavering slightly.

Alvin reached out, gently taking her hand in his. "I understand, Jenna. I know how you are. Always a perfectionist. But I want you to know that I would never purposefully stress you out."

Jenna felt tears prick at the corners of her eyes, moved by his heartfelt words. "I know, Alvin. I don't want anything to come between us, especially not a silly misunderstanding."

Alvin squeezed her hand reassuringly. "I don't want that either, Jenna. You mean too much to me." His eyes searched hers, the depth of his feelings evident in his gaze.

Jenna's heart swelled, the warmth of his touch spreading through her like a soothing balm. "Friends?" she asked him.

Alvin smiled and nodded. "Always."

Chapter Nine

The church buzzed with activity as Jenna helped arrange the poinsettias near the altar. She stepped back, admiring the riot of red petals against the evergreen garlands. Christmas Eve had always been her favorite service of the year at this little church in her hometown.

"Those flowers look perfect, Jenna," said Pastor Greer as he approached, his kind eyes crinkling at the corners. "I'm so glad you're here to help us get ready."

Jenna smiled. "I wouldn't miss it." She blinked back the sudden prick of tears.

Greer patted her shoulder. "We've missed having you here too. Will you be sharing a testimony tonight during the service? I know folks would love to hear from you."

Jenna hesitated. Public speaking usually didn't phase her, but baring her soul in front of everyone she'd grown up with felt different somehow. More raw and exposed.

"I'm not sure what I would even say," she admitted.

"Speak from your heart," Greer advised gently. "Share what God has been teaching you this year. How He's worked in your life."

Jenna nodded slowly. "Alright. I'll do it."

As the sun set in a lilac sky outside the stained glass, the pews filled with familiar faces, awash in candlelight. Jenna's hands shook slightly as she made her way to the podium. She took a deep breath.

"I've learned a lot about myself this past year," Jenna began. "About what truly matters. That as much as I've chased success and validation through my career, my deepest longings can only be met in God."

Her eyes shone with unshed tears as she continued. "Being back here, I'm remembering what it means to belong. To be part of a loving community. To walk in faith over fear. And I'm realizing that I don't have to have it all figured out. I just need to trust God with each step."

"So this Christmas, I'm laying down my need for

control, my impossible expectations for myself. And I'm embracing the unshakable hope and peace we have in Jesus—the greatest gift of all."

As Jenna finished, a holy hush filled the room. Then, as one, the congregation rose in a standing ovation, many brushing away tears. In that moment, Jenna felt a deep settling in her soul.

Her eyes met Alvin's, and it humbled her to see his glistening with tears.

He looked *proud* of her, and that pleased her more than she ever thought possible.

She was *home*.

After the service, Jenna found herself drawn to the flickering candles lining the altar. She closed her eyes, savoring the stillness that enveloped the now-empty church. The soft shuffling of footsteps caused her to turn, and she found herself face-to-face with Alvin.

"Jenna," he breathed, his blue eyes filled with warmth. "Your words tonight...they touched so many hearts. Including mine."

Jenna felt a lump form in her throat. "Alvin, I..." She paused, gathering her courage. "I owe you an apology. For the way I left things all those years ago. I was so focused on my own dreams that I didn't consider how it would affect you. Or what I was leaving behind."

Alvin reached out, gently taking her hand. "I forgave you long ago, Jenna. I always understood your need to chase your dreams. I just wished I could have been a part of them."

Tears spilled down Jenna's cheeks. "I'm so sorry, Alvin. I thought I needed to prove myself out there. But being back here, with you...I'm realizing that my heart never really left."

Alvin's thumb brushed away a tear. "Jenna, I've never stopped loving you. And if you'll have me, I want to be part of your life again. Here, in the city, wherever God leads us."

Jenna's heart swelled with love and gratitude. "I'd like that," she whispered. "More than anything."

As they stood there, hands intertwined, the candlelight casting a warm glow over their faces, Jenna felt a profound sense of peace wash over her. She was exactly where she was meant to be. In the glow of God's love, and the promise of a future with the man who had always held her heart.

She gazed at Alvin.

He gazed at her.

And then, as if drawn by an invisible force, Jenna

and Alvin slowly leaned towards each other, their faces mere inches apart. The twinkling lights strung along the church's exterior cast a magical glow over the moment, as if the heavens themselves were smiling upon their rekindled connection.

Alvin's hand gently cupped Jenna's cheek, his thumb caressing her soft skin. "You're so beautiful," he murmured, his voice barely above a whisper. "Inside and out."

Jenna's heart raced, her pulse thrumming with anticipation. She could feel the warmth of Alvin's breath, the nearness of his presence igniting a spark deep within her soul. "Alvin," she breathed, her eyes fluttering closed.

And then, with a tenderness that spoke volumes of his love, Alvin closed the distance between them, pressing his lips to hers in a gentle, reverent kiss. Jenna melted into his embrace, her arms winding around his neck as she surrendered to the overwhelming sensation of coming home.

The kiss deepened, years of longing and unspoken emotions pouring forth in a symphony of passion. Jenna's heart soared, her spirit singing with the knowledge that this was where she truly belonged —in the arms of the man who had never stopped loving her, even when she had lost sight of what mattered most.

As they parted, breathless and flushed, Alvin rested his forehead against hers. "Merry Christmas, Jenna," he whispered, his eyes shining with adoration.

Jenna smiled, her heart overflowing with joy and gratitude. "Merry Christmas, Alvin," she replied, knowing that this was just the beginning of a beautiful new chapter in their story—one written by the hand of God, and sealed with a kiss under the Christmas lights.

Chapter Ten

Jenna stood on the back porch of her parents' Florida home, a steaming mug of coffee nestled in her hands as she watched the sun peek above the horizon, painting the sky in hues of orange and pink. The gentle breeze carried the scent of salt and sand, a reminder of the beautiful moments she'd shared with Alvin over the past week.

Her heart swelled with the memory of his tender embrace, the way his eyes sparkled when he laughed at her silly jokes. She couldn't deny the connection they shared, the way he made her feel whole and understood like no one else ever had.

But doubt crept in like an unwelcome guest, whispering that a long-distance relationship could never work, not with her demanding career waiting for her back in New York.

The screen door creaked open behind her, and Jenna turned to see her mother stepping out onto the porch, a knowing smile on her face. "Penny for your thoughts, sweetheart?"

Jenna sighed, taking a sip of her coffee. "Just thinking about...everything. Alvin, my job, how I'm supposed to make this work."

Her mother nodded, leaning against the railing beside her. "I know it seems daunting, honey. But if there's one thing I've learned in life, it's that when you find something precious, you fight for it. Don't let fear hold you back from what could be the greatest adventure of your life."

Jenna felt tears prick at the corners of her eyes. "But what if I mess it up? What if I can't balance my career and a relationship?"

"Oh, Jenna." Her mother wrapped an arm around her shoulders, pulling her close. "You're stronger than you give yourself credit for. And if Alvin is the man I think he is, he'll be right there beside you, supporting you every step of the way. Trust in your heart, and in God's plan for you."

Jenna leaned into her mother's embrace, feeling a sense of peace wash over her. Maybe, just maybe, she could have it all—the career she'd worked so hard for, and the love she'd always dreamed of. All she had to do was take a leap of faith.

Jenna stood on the church steps, her heart racing as she watched Alvin approach. The sunlight caught in his dark hair, making his blue eyes shine even brighter. He smiled at her, that warm, gentle smile that never failed to make her melt.

"Hey there," he said softly, reaching for her hand. "I was hoping I'd find you here."

Jenna laced her fingers through his, reveling in the warmth of his touch. "I needed some time to think," she admitted. "About...everything."

Alvin nodded, his thumb tracing small circles on the back of her hand. "I know it's a lot to take in. Your life in New York, your career...and then there's us."

"I don't want to lose you," Jenna whispered, her voice catching. "But I'm scared, Alvin. Scared of making the wrong choice, of letting people down."

He turned to face her fully, his free hand coming up to cup her cheek. "Jenna, you could never let me down. I love you, every part of you. Your strength, your passion, your determination. I don't want you to give up your dreams for me."

Jenna leaned into his touch, her eyes fluttering closed. "But what if I want a new dream? One that includes you?"

Alvin's breath hitched, his eyes widening. "Jenna, are you saying...?"

She nodded, a smile blooming on her face. "I already talked to the office. I can keep my job and work remotely—from here. I want to stay, Alvin. I want to be with you, to build a life here. I know it won't be easy, but I'm ready to take that leap of faith."

His answering grin was blinding, joy radiating from every inch of him. "I was hoping you'd say that," he murmured, reaching into his pocket. "Because I have something I want to ask you."

Jenna's heart skipped a beat as Alvin dropped to one knee, a small velvet box in his hand. "Jenna Livingston, you are the most incredible woman I have ever met. Your love has brought so much light into my life, and I can't imagine spending another day without you by my side. Will you marry me?"

Tears streamed down Jenna's face as she nodded, her voice caught in her throat. "Yes," she managed, her smile wobbling. "Yes, Alvin, I'll marry you."

He slipped the ring onto her finger, a simple band adorned with a sparkling diamond. It was perfect, just like him. Alvin rose to his feet, pulling her into his arms and capturing her lips in a searing kiss.

As they stood there, wrapped in each other's embrace, Jenna knew she had made the right choice.

Jenna pulled back from the kiss, her eyes shining with unshed tears. She gazed into Alvin's face, taking in every beloved feature. His strong jawline, the gentle curve of his lips, the way his eyes crinkled at the corners when he smiled. She raised a hand to cup his cheek, marveling at the fact that this incredible man had chosen her.

"I love you," she whispered, her voice thick with emotion. "I love you so much."

Alvin turned his head to press a kiss into her palm. "I love you too, Jenna. Truth be told, I always have. I've prayed for a long time you would come back."

Jenna was humbled by his admission. All this time...Alvin had put his life on hold, waiting for her, trusting in God that He would send her back to him.

And He had.

They stood there for a long moment, simply holding each other, basking in the warmth of their love. Around them, the church was quiet, the only sound the soft whisper of their breathing.

Finally, Alvin pulled back, taking Jenna's hand in his. "We should probably tell your family the good news," he said, a mischievous twinkle in his eye.

Jenna laughed, the sound bright and joyful. "They're going to be thrilled," she said, squeezing his hand. "I think they've been rooting for us from the start."

Hand in hand, they made their way out of the church, ready to share their happiness with the world. As they stepped into the sunlight, Jenna felt a sense of peace wash over her. This was where she was meant to be, by Alvin's side, building a life together in this beautiful little town.

She knew there would be challenges ahead. Merging their lives wouldn't be easy, and there would be sacrifices to be made. But with Alvin by her side, she knew they could face anything.

For the first time in a long time, Jenna felt truly at peace. She had found her home, her heart, and her future.

Chapter Eleven

Jenna and Alvin strolled along the shore, the sand sifting beneath their feet. The sun danced on the ocean, casting a golden glow on their faces. Alvin turned to Jenna, his blue eyes filled with warmth. "I've been thinking a lot about the future lately."

Jenna smiled, her hazel eyes sparkling. "Me too. It's funny how everything seems to fall into place when you're in the right place."

"Absolutely." Alvin nodded. "I've always dreamed of making a real difference in people's lives. Working with the church and the community has shown me that it's possible."

"I know what you mean," Jenna replied. "Back in

New York, I was so focused on climbing the corporate ladder. But here, I feel like I'm part of something bigger. Something that truly matters."

They sat down on a nearby bench, their hands intertwined. Alvin's voice was soft yet filled with conviction. "I want to keep serving others, to help this community thrive. And I can't imagine doing it without you by my side."

Jenna's heart swelled with love and purpose. "I feel the same way, Alvin. Your dedication and faith inspire me every day. Together, we can make a real impact."

As they discussed their shared dreams, Jenna marveled at how perfectly their aspirations aligned. It was as if their paths had been destined to converge all along.

The following week, Jenna and Alvin joined a local mission trip to help rebuild homes for families in need. As they worked side by side, hammering nails and painting walls, their bond deepened with each passing moment.

During a break, Alvin wiped the sweat from his brow and grinned at Jenna. "You know, I never thought I'd find someone who shared my passion for serving others so completely."

Jenna laughed, her face smudged with paint. "I guess God had a plan for us all along."

"He certainly did." Alvin's eyes shone with love and admiration.

As they continued their work, Jenna felt a profound sense of fulfillment. Every smile from a grateful family, every word of encouragement from Alvin, and every whispered prayer strengthened her faith and resolve.

In the evenings, they gathered with the other volunteers, sharing stories and reflections. The laughter and camaraderie filled Jenna's heart with joy. She had never felt so connected, so alive.

Alvin wrapped an arm around her shoulders, his voice filled with emotion. "This is what it's all about, isn't it? Serving God and loving others."

Jenna leaned into his embrace, her heart overflowing with gratitude. "It is. And I'm so blessed to be sharing this journey with you."

As they looked out at the community they had helped to rebuild, Jenna knew that this was just the beginning. Together, she and Alvin would continue to live out their faith, making a difference one act of love at a time.

The town square buzzed with excitement as residents gathered to celebrate Jenna and Alvin's engagement. Colorful streamers danced in the gentle breeze, and the aroma of freshly baked goods wafted through the air. Jenna's heart swelled with emotion as she took in the sea of smiling faces, each one a testament to the love and support of their close-knit community.

Alvin's hand found hers, his warm touch a reassuring anchor amidst the joyful chaos. "Can you believe they did all this for us?" he whispered, his voice filled with awe.

Jenna squeezed his hand, a radiant smile lighting up her face. "It's amazing. I never knew love could feel this wonderful."

As they made their way through the crowd, friends and neighbors showered them with hugs and well-wishes. Old Mrs. Hawkins pressed a lovingly crafted quilt into Jenna's arms, her eyes twinkling with wisdom. "May this keep you warm on the coldest of nights, and remind you of the love that surrounds you."

Jenna hugged the quilt close, deeply touched by the gesture. "Thank you so much, Mrs. Hawkins. It's beautiful."

The celebration continued with laughter, music,

and heartfelt speeches. Pastor Greer took the stage, his voice filled with warmth and conviction. "Jenna and Alvin, your love and dedication to each other and to this community have been an inspiration to us all. May God continue to bless your journey together, and may you always find strength in your faith and in the love that surrounds you."

Tears of joy streamed down Jenna's face as she leaned into Alvin's embrace. In that moment, she knew that she had found her true home—not just in this charming Florida town, but in the love and faith that bound her heart to Alvin's.

As the sun began to set, casting a golden glow over the festivities, Alvin led Jenna to the center of the square. He took her hands in his, his eyes shining with love and promise. "Jenna, I know our journey is just beginning, but I already know that a lifetime with you will be the greatest adventure of all."

Jenna's heart soared, her voice trembling with emotion. "I feel the same way, Alvin. With you by my side and God in our hearts, I know that anything is possible."

As they swayed to the gentle music, surrounded by the love and support of their community, Jenna and Alvin knew that they had found something truly special. Their path ahead might not always be easy, but with faith, love, and each other, they were ready to face whatever the future might bring.

Excerpt from the next book in the
A Very Merry State of
Love series

CHRISTMAS IN KENTUCKY

Courtney Rivera's heels clicked against the weathered wood of her grandmother's front porch. As she fumbled for the key, her gaze settled on the faded rocking chair where her grandmother had spent countless evenings spinning tales and sharing life lessons. A lump formed in Courtney's throat as she pushed open the door.

Inside, the familiar scent of cinnamon and vanilla wrapped around her like a warm hug. Courtney set down her designer suitcase, taking in the cozy living room with its crocheted afghans and framed family photos. Memories flooded back—summers spent chasing fireflies, winters curled up by the hearth listening to Aunt her grandmother's soothing voice recite Bible verses.

"Oh Grandma," Courtney whispered, a tear sliding down her cheek. "I miss you so much already."

She wandered into the kitchen, trailing her fingers along the countertop. In her mind's eye, she could see her grandmother, apron tied snugly around her waist, humming hymns as she rolled out dough for apple pies. The ache in Courtney's chest intensified.

"Why did I stay away so long?" she murmured, guilt tugging at her heartstrings. The fast pace of city life had consumed her, leaving little time for visits home. Now, standing amidst the remnants of her grandmother's love, Courtney yearned for the simplicity and comfort of her childhood.

With a sigh, she opened the fridge, smiling wistfully at the containers of her grandmother's famous chicken and dumplings. Courtney knew each dish was prepared with a prayer and a sprinkle of faith. She grabbed a Tupperware, suddenly ravenous for a taste of home.

As she sat at the worn wooden table, savoring each bite, Courtney's mind drifted to simpler times —lazy afternoons shelling peas on the porch swing, giggling with her grandmother over glasses of sweet tea. A pang of longing pierced her heart.

"I don't know if I'm cut out for the corporate world anymore," she admitted aloud, her voice echoing in the empty kitchen. "My soul feels so weary, Grandma. What would you tell me to do?"

In the silence, Courtney could almost hear her grandmother's gentle wisdom: *Listen to your heart, sweet pea. The Lord will guide your path.*

With a deep breath, Courtney cleared her plate and wandered out onto the back porch. The rolling Kentucky hills stretched before her. She inhaled the crisp air, feeling a sense of peace wash over her troubled spirit.

Maybe, just maybe, this trip home would help her rediscover what truly mattered. With a whispered prayer, Courtney surrendered her uncertainties to the One who had always been her strength. Her grandmother's love, even from heaven, would light the way.

The crunch of tires on gravel pulled Courtney from her reverie. A familiar old pickup truck rolled to a stop in front of the house, its faded blue paint a testament to years of hard work. The driver's door swung open, and a tall figure emerged, his broad shoulders stretching a well-worn flannel shirt.

"Tony Turner, as I live and breathe," Courtney called out, a smile tugging at her lips. She stepped off the porch, memories of childhood adventures flooding her mind.

"Well, if it isn't Courtney Rivera, the big-city hotshot," Tony teased, his blue eyes crinkling at the corners. He strode over, enveloping her in a warm hug that smelled of earth and sunshine. "Welcome home, Court."

Courtney melted into the embrace, surprised by the sudden rush of emotions. "It's good to be back," she murmured, blinking away the sting of tears. "I just wish it were under better circumstances."

Tony pulled back, his calloused hands resting gently on her shoulders. "I'm so sorry about your grandma, Courtney. She was a special lady."

"She sure was," Courtney agreed, her voice catching. She cleared her throat, desperate to change the subject. "So, what brings you out this way?"

"Oh, you know, just helping the Johnsons with their post-harvest clean-up," Tony shrugged, his gaze drifting to the fields beyond. "It's been a long season, but we're all pitching in to get things squared away before winter hits."

Courtney nodded, a pang of guilt niggling at her heart. Here she was, worrying about her own problems, while her childhood friend spent his days serving others. "That's really kind of you, Tony. I'm sure they appreciate the help."

"Ah, it's nothing," he waved off the praise, a hint of a blush creeping up his neck. "Just doing what needs to be done. That's the way it is around here."

An awkward silence stretched between them, the weight of years apart suddenly palpable. Courtney scuffed the toe of her designer boot against the gravel, searching for the right words.

"So, how's life in the big city treating you?" Tony finally asked, his tone light but his eyes searching. "I bet it's a far cry from this little old town."

Courtney laughed, a brittle sound even to her own ears. "Oh, you know, it's...it's something else. Always busy, always rushing. Sometimes I wonder if I'm really living, or just existing."

The words hung heavy in the air, an admission she hadn't even made to herself. Tony studied her face, his expression softening with understanding.

"I know what you mean," he said quietly, his gaze drifting to the horizon. "There are days when I wonder if I'm doing the right thing, staying here on the farm. If maybe I should've followed a different path, like you did."

Courtney's heart clenched at the wistfulness in his voice. She reached out, her hand finding his, rough and warm. "You're doing important work here, Tony. This community needs people like you, with roots that run deep and a heart that gives endlessly."

He smiled then, a genuine, lopsided grin that transported Courtney back to summers spent chasing fireflies and whispering secrets in the hayloft. "And the world needs people like you, Courtney. People who dream big and chase their passions, no matter where they lead."

They stood there, hands clasped, as the golden light of late afternoon bathed the farmyard in a gentle glow. For a moment, the years melted away, and Courtney felt a flicker of something long-forgotten stir in her soul.

Award-winning author Kayla Lowe writes women's fiction that explores complex themes with sensitivity and depth. Kayla's books delve into the intricacies of relationships, self-discovery, and resilience. From cozy love stories interspersed with a bit of faith to heartwarming tales of friendship and suspenseful novels of empowerment and heartbreak, her books illustrate the struggles specific to women.

When she's not churning out her next novel, you can find her with her feet in the sand and a book in her hand or curled up on the couch with her dogs.

Visit her website at www.authorkaylalowe.com.

A Courtship in Covent Garden

Whispers in Westminster

Romance in Regent's Park

Serenade on Strand Street

Treasure in Tower Bridge

<u>Sweet Honey by the Sea</u>

<u>The Beekeeper's Secret (Book 1)</u>

<u>A Royal Honeycomb (Book 2)</u>

<u>Bees in Blossom (Book 3)</u>

<u>Honeyed Kisses (Book 4)</u>

<u>Blooming Forever (Book 5)</u>

<u>Strawberry Beach Series</u>

<u>Beachside Lessons (Book 1)</u>

<u>Beachside Lessons (Book 2)</u>

<u>Beachside Lessons (Book 3)</u>

Panama City Beach Series

Sun-Kissed Secrets (Book 1)

Sun-Kissed Secrets (Book 2)

Sun-Kissed Secrets (Book 3)

The Tainted Love Saga

Of Love and Deception (Book 1)

Of Love and Family (Book 2)

Of Love and Violence (Book 3)

Of Love and Abuse(Book 4)

Of Love and Crime (Book 5)

Of Love and Addiction (Book 6)

Of Love and Redemption (Book 7)

<u>Standalones</u>

Maiden's Blush

<u>Poetry</u>

Phantom Poetry

Lost and Found